HARPER
AND THE
Scarlet Umbrella

For all of my family, who made my childhood bright.
And for wonderful Amelie, who makes the magic real.
With special thanks to Alasdair Malloy and The Royal
Liverpool Philharmonic Orchestra.
C.B.

For the beautiful Marie. A magical musician and
wonderful sister xxx
L.E.A.

Text copyright © Cerrie Burnell, 2015
Illustrations copyright © Laura Ellen Anderson, 2015

First published in the United Kingdom by Scholastic Children's Books, an
imprint of Scholastic Ltd, 2015.
This hardcover edition published by Sky Pony Press, 2017.
This is a work of fiction. Names, characters, places, and incidents are from the
author's imagination and used fictitiously.
Sky Pony Press books may be purchased in bulk at special discounts for
sales promotion, corporate gifts, fund-raising, or educational purposes. Special
editions can also be created to specifications. For details, contact the Special
Sales Department, Sky Pony Press, 307 West 36th Street, 11th Floor, New York,
NY 10018 or info@skyhorsepublishing.com.
Sky Pony® is a registered trademark of Skyhorse Publishing, Inc.®, a Delaware
corporation.

Visit our website at www.skyponypress.com
Books, authors, and more at www.skyponypressblog.com

10 9 8 7 6 5 4 3 2 1

Library of Congress Control Number: 2016958558

Jacket illustration © Laura Ellen Anderson
Jacket design by Andrew Biscomb

Hardcover ISBN: 978-1-5107-1566-0
EBook ISBN: 978-1-5107-1568-4

Printed in the United States of America

HARPER
AND THE
Scarlet Umbrella

CERRIE BURNELL

Illustrated by Laura Ellen Anderson

Sky Pony Press
New York

Once there was a girl called Harper who had a rare musical gift. She heard songs on the wind, rhythms on the rain, and hope in the beat of a butterfly's wing. Harper could play every instrument she ever picked up, without learning a single note. Sometimes late at night, alone with her cat, Midnight, Harper heard a melody that made her heart stand still. For it seemed that it came from the stars themselves. . . .

Chapter One
THE BROKEN UMBRELLA

From the fourteenth floor of the Tall Apartment Block, Harper gazed dreamily across the City of Clouds. Trolleys rumbled through heavy rain and bright umbrellas bobbed like little boats.

"Darling, I'm leaving with the Dutch Opera House in ten minutes sharp," Great

Aunt Sassy cooed, as she stitched a pink petticoat into a gorgeous twirly gown. "They're picking me up by helicopter."

Harper smiled and put her arms around her Great Aunt Sassy's large waist, the scent of lavender tickling her nose. Sassy

Miller was the chief dressmaker for the Dutch Opera House. It was her job to sew hems, knit hats, and create fabulous dresses.

Every four weeks, when the moon was round and full, Great Aunt Sassy traveled to Holland to check on all her beautiful gowns. Harper secretly liked it when Great Aunt Sassy went away, as she got to stay with the other residents of the Tall Apartment Block. Tonight she was staying with strange old Elsie Caraham, who lived on the topmost floor. Tomorrow she was with Madame Flora at the ballet school, on floor three.

The sound of a whirring helicopter filled the little flat. "My ride has arrived!" Great

Aunt Sassy cheered, seizing her suitcase and charging out the door.

Harper ran to catch up with her, grabbing her yellow umbrella as she went. As they stepped onto the rooftop, a Heartbeat of rain drummed from the sky. Harper hardly noticed. In the City of Clouds it rained every day, in many different ways, pouring down water that was good enough to drink.

There was:

Summer Dew: a light rain that barely touched you.

Sea Mist: a soft rain that emerged from the air like fog.

Heartbeat: an even rain, steady as your

heart.

Cloudburst: a downpour that soaked you to the skin.

Icefall: a hard rain that struck like hail.

Thunder Break: when the sky was alive with storms.

"Have a weekend as wonderful as you." Sassy beamed, kissing Harper's forehead and struggling into the helicopter.

"I will." Harper giggled, her mind already skipping at the thought of the fun she was going to have.

But as the helicopter spun into the clouds, the force from its propellers snatched Harper's yellow umbrella and tossed it into the air. Harper gave a squeal as it was thrown in a puddle at her feet, badly torn.

From the sky above, Great Aunt Sassy peered down and almost dropped her teacup.

"Whatever will we do?" she groaned. "Everyone in the City of Clouds owns an umbrella and now Harper's is ruined." She leaned through the swaths of swirling cloud, took a deep breath and then— knowing that Harper's life would change forever—called, "Darling, you must use the Scarlet Umbrella. It was left to you by . . ."

But Great Aunt Sassy's words were stolen away by the wind. Harper was alone, a little girl on a rooftop with a broken umbrella.

Chapter Two
THE BIRDCAGE

Harper blinked in amazement as the rain lightened to a soft Summer Dew. She stared at her reflection in a puddle. A girl with pale skin, dark hair, and eyes the color of a winter sea gazed back at her with a big smile. "I can use the Scarlet Umbrella," Harper said excitedly.

She darted down the stairs, through the door of their little flat, and into the bathroom. A shiver of excitement danced over Harper's skin. In the corner of the bathroom stood an enormous birdcage. Locked inside its slim white bars was an umbrella of magnificent scarlet silk.

So often had Harper dreamed of opening the birdcage, but Great Aunt Sassy had never allowed her to, insisting that the Scarlet Umbrella was too old and fragile to use. Carefully, Harper picked up a tiny golden key, which hung above the sink. It had been there for as long as Harper could remember, shining through her memories like a key to forgotten secrets. Gently, she turned the key and with a click the birdcage was open. Harper held her breath and lifted the umbrella out. It burst open in her hands, making her jump and laugh all at once! It really was quite splendid—like a prop from one of Great Aunt Sassy's operas. "It weighs nothing at

all." Harper smiled, for it felt as if she were holding a handful of feathers, and though it was very old, the umbrella didn't seem fragile at all.

"Midnight!" Harper yelled, tearing around the little flat. "Midnight, come and see my amazing umbrella."

But Midnight was nowhere to be found. Harper pulled a small piccolo flute from her pocket and played Midnight's favorite melody. But still he did not appear. She peeked beneath the table and noticed something very odd. Midnight's bowl of cream and peppermint mouse had not been touched. A whisper of worry crept into Harper's heart.

You see, Midnight wasn't quite like any

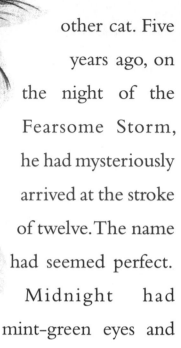

other cat. Five years ago, on the night of the Fearsome Storm, he had mysteriously arrived at the stroke of twelve. The name had seemed perfect.

Midnight had mint-green eyes and jet-black fur with snow-white paws and a white-tipped tail. Wherever Harper wandered, Midnight would follow, three paces behind. Sometimes, when Great Aunt Sassy took Harper to the ballet or to the movies, Midnight would already be there, curled happily in Harper's seat.

How he guessed where she was going to sit, nobody ever knew.

Harper stood in the middle of the flat, breathing in the scent of lavender and listening to a lullaby of sad Summer Dew rain. And suddenly, Harper felt terribly lonely. "Where are you, Midnight?" she whispered . . . and that's when the magical thing happened.

Chapter Three
THE MAGICAL THING

Without any warning, the Scarlet
Umbrella shot out of Harper's hand and
flew toward the door. With a light crash,
it hit the handle and slid to the floor,
landing like a beach umbrella. Harper
stood perfectly still, too stunned to move.
Then her heart soared. "You're magic!"

she cried, swinging the umbrella into the air.

Its handle was silver and smooth. Harper clutched it tightly, pressed her eyes shut and whispered, "Will you help me find Midnight?" At first, nothing happened. Then the funniest feeling came over Harper, a feeling she'd had before in a dream. A feeling of being lighter than clouds and drifting past the moon. Slowly, she opened a single sea-gray eye and found she was floating.

Harper was so surprised, she let go of the Scarlet Umbrella and started falling toward the table. Quicker than lightning, the umbrella flipped upside down and caught Harper in its dome. "You can fly!" She laughed, leaping out and dancing around the apartment. The umbrella gave a tiny quiver, as if it understood. Harper

reached up and took it by the handle, as if she was taking someone's hand.

"Let's find Midnight." She smiled and set off at a run, her feet dusting the stairs as lightly as snow.

On the seventh floor, Harper and the Scarlet Umbrella paused. Carnival music echoed through the stairwells. "The Lucases must be having a party." Harper beamed, banging on a bright orange door. The Lucas family were a troupe of percussionists from sunny Brazil. They owned every drum you could think of and never seemed to sleep.

"Welcome, Harper!" called Mariana Lucas, who was wearing a garland of flowers in her hair. Her husband, Paulo, was in the kitchen, frying fish. The twins, Augusto and Luciano, were juggling, and Isabella was performing a samba routine.

"I'm eighteen today!" Isabella screamed, pulling Harper into a hug.

"Happy birthday!" Harper yelled. "Is Midnight here?"

At once, the room went silent and Harper felt a coldness sweep over her skin. Liliana Lucas, who was only three, began to sob. "Katarina's gone missing," she wept. Katarina was the Lucas family's beloved cat.

"Perhaps Katarina and Midnight are having an adventure together?" said Isabella brightly. But Harper wasn't so sure.

On the fifth floor, the Scarlet Umbrella came to rest outside a flat so crowded with books it could have been a library. Papers, postcards, and half-finished poems spilled across the floor. Liesel, the littlest member of the German family, was busily playing with a string of paper mice. Ferdie, her older brother, was lounging on the sofa, trying to read a serious play.

"Good morning, Harper!" called their mother, Brigitte, offering Harper a pretzel.

"Good morning, Little Harp," called Peter, their father, who was a famous German writer.

Harper gave Peter a wave and peered into his wonderfully messy study. The thought of all the new stories being typed brightened her heart.

"Is Midnight here?" she asked hopefully.

"No, and nor is Ludo," said Liesel coolly. Liesel was small with tangled blonde hair and filthy nails. She loathed cats but loved mice. It was a great relief to her that cats were going missing.

Ferdie, her brother, gave a serious frown and threw down his play. "Ludo has left us and we don't know why."

Harper swallowed anxiously. "I think Midnight's m–missing, too," she stammered. Ferdie leaped up from the sofa and flung an arm around Harper's shoulders.

"Midnight would never leave you," he said confidently. "I promise you he will come back."

On the third floor, the Scarlet Umbrella leaned softly toward the ballet school. Harper, Ferdie, Liesel, and her string of paper mice slipped through the door.

Madame Flora sat alone at the cherry-wood piano. Harper's fingers longed to stroke its ivory keys. But, instead, she found herself scanning the dance studio for Snowflake, the ballet school's cat.

She stared sadly at the empty basket. "Is Midnight here?" she asked quietly.

Madame Flora's face became pale with sorrow. She folded her arms across her chest like two graceful wings. "No," she whispered. "Nor is Snowflake."

Harper sighed and blew Madame Flora a kiss goodbye. Ferdie gave her a swift bow and Liesel bobbed a little curtsy, which was so perfect that for a moment it made Madame Flora smile. Then the three children and the paper mice were gone.

Cats across the City of Clouds were disappearing. Something had to be done.

Chapter Four
MIDNIGHT MUSIC

Elsie Caraham was the oldest resident in the Tall Apartment Block. She owned a wonderful collection of violas that she often let Harper play. But tonight, they were making no sound at all. Tonight, Harper and Elsie were listening.

They perched on the rooftop beneath

a canopy of storm blooms—flowers that only bloom in the rain. Harper was curled beneath the Scarlet Umbrella, her dark hair tucked away, her ears open. Elsie was huddled in an emerald-green cape that matched her emerald-green eyes, making her look like a fairy-tale witch.

"When the clock chimes twelve, a strange music starts up and all the cats follow it," Elsie hissed softly. "Most of them never return."

Elsie was furious that her own two cats, Memphis and Tallulah, had vanished, too. *Cats are as much a part of the city as the clouds are*, thought Harper. The only household she knew of that didn't have a cat was the Nathanielsons, on the tenth floor. They had a wolf, instead. Not a wicked wolf, or a wild wolf, or a wolf you might find in a magical wood. But a strange, intelligent creature with glowing golden eyes.

The wolf belonged to Nate Nathanielson. Nate was visually impaired, and could only see lightness or dark. He had found the wolf as a cub, mistaken her for a dog, and brought her home. The wolf had remained at his side ever since.

An odd note of music sliced through the air and Harper forgot about Nate and his wolf. She strained her ears to listen. From somewhere below the rooftops and above the cellars came a strange lilting tune. It was music like nothing Harper or Elsie had ever dreamed of. Music that could steal your soul.

Elsie raised her spyglass to her unusually bright eyes and peered through the Sea Mist rain. "Look!" she cried wildly.

Harper squinted through the spyglass and froze. Cats of every shape and size were prowling across the city.

"They're headed for the Unforgotten Concert Hall—in our basement!" Elsie croaked.

Harper leaped to her feet. "I have to find them," she said boldly.

Elsie's eyes twinkled like stolen emeralds. Then she winked and said, "Go!" Harper fled from the rooftop.

As she dashed down the stairs, she noticed that the Tall Apartment Block seemed different in the dark. Shadows moved of their own accord. Late night chatter floated all around. Far away, someone was dancing.

But Harper wasn't afraid. This was her home—she knew every inch of it. Especially the Unforgotten Concert Hall; it was one of her favorite places. Its front entrance was on the street, but the hall, itself, and its cobweb-laced dressing rooms were in the basement of the Tall Apartment Block.

Harper tried the stage door. It was locked. Then she spotted a small, grimy window, just a little bit taller than her. *If I could just reach it*, she thought.

No sooner had the thought danced through her mind than the Scarlet Umbrella rose up high, pulling Harper with it, so she was eye-level with the window. She took a breath and peered through the dirt.

Inside stood a terrifyingly tall man in a sweeping satin coat. His hair was the color of magpie feathers. His nose crooked as a wizard's. His skin as brown as fallen leaves. But all Harper saw was the cat he carried in his arms.

"Midnight!" she cried, and her voice, so much louder than she intended, rang out as clear as a nightingale's.

Midnight gave a fierce meow. The terrifyingly tall man spun around in fury. For an awful moment, Harper found herself gazing into two hateful brown eyes. Then the Scarlet Umbrella whisked her away, up the stairs, and back to safety, her heart beating like a bird inside a cage.

They didn't slow down until they reached the tenth floor. Then the Scarlet Umbrella lowered Harper to the ground and she sank onto the stairs, trying to gather her scattered thoughts. What was the terrifyingly tall man doing with Midnight? Where was that bewitching music coming from? And how was she going to rescue Midnight and all the other cats? Something growled in the darkness and Harper's blood turned cold. There, in the murky gloom of the stairwell, glowed the golden eyes of a wolf.

Chapter Five
THE BOY AND THE WOLF

The wolf gave a low warning growl. Harper almost let out a scream.

Then she saw a boy step from the shadows.

"Don't worry. You just gave her a scare," said Nate Nathanielson calmly.

Harper wilted with relief and smiled,

then blushed, remembering that Nate probably couldn't see her smiling.

Nate's skin was deep brown but his eyes were as clouded as morning fog. People thought the wolf was like a guide dog. But as Harper stared at the fierce and beautiful creature at Nate's side, she wasn't so sure. The wolf wasn't on a leash.

"I didn't mean to startle her," said Harper shyly.

"It's okay," said Nate. "Your feet made no sound. If it wasn't for your shadow I wouldn't have known you were there."

For a moment, Harper was still. She looked at the boy and the wolf, wondering if she dare tell them about the Scarlet Umbrella and the missing cats. She had

known Nate all her life, but never really spoken to him. She'd wanted to make friends before, but something about the wolf made her fall silent.

She gripped the umbrella closely and said, "The reason you didn't hear my footsteps is because I was floating."

She expected Nate to laugh. But he put his head to one side as if he were thinking.

"It's my umbrella," Harper continued. "It's very old and sort of enchanted!"

Nate reached out and ran his hands over the scarlet silk. "It feels powerful and strong," he said quietly.

"It is," Harper smiled, her eyes lighting up with an idea. "Would you like to try it?"

For a moment, Nate hesitated. Then the wolf raised her head and padded softly over to Harper. Harper didn't dare move. The wolf didn't touch her, but lay at her feet and gave a growl so soft it sounded like a purr.

"Smoke seems to think it's a good idea."

Nate grinned.

"Smoke . . ." Harper murmured. It was a wonderful name for her. The wolf's fur shimmered, as if she was made out of mist. "Come on then," Harper cried and they set off for the rooftop.

Elsie had gone back inside so the children and the wolf found themselves alone beneath a sky of silvery stars.

"You have to hold the handle tight," said Harper, passing the umbrella to Nate.

She closed her own hands over his. "On the count of three," she whispered. "One, two, thr—" and the umbrella shot into the air.

Smoke's wild eyes flashed and she gave a surprised snarl. But neither of the children

noticed. They were having too much fun.

"It's like we're part of the sky," Nate said, laughing as the umbrella swept across the rooftop.

"Like we're made of night-clouds," Harper agreed. Then Icefall rain started to rattle down on them, making the umbrella shake like a boat on the waves.

With a happy shriek, Harper brought the umbrella to land. The children and the wolf dashed beneath a canopy of storm blooms. Nate rubbed the wolf's ears until she lay at his feet like a puppy, but Harper noticed her eyes were open wide. *Smoke is not Nate's guide dog*, she thought. *She is his best friend, just like Midnight and me.* And she told Nate all about Midnight, the missing cats, and the man with magpie-feather hair.

"I think what we need to do," said Nate, "is come up with a plan." As the Icefall rain thinned to a Heartbeat drizzle and the storm blooms opened their dusky gray petals, a plan began to form.

Chapter Six
A TRIP TO THE UNFORGOTTEN CONCERT HALL

The next morning, Harper hugged Elsie goodbye and hurried to the tenth floor where Nate and Smoke were waiting.

Ferdie's sharp German accent echoed up the stairs. "Ludo's been missing two days! Don't you care?"

"No, I don't!" yelled Liesel, flicking a chunk of dirty hair out of her eyes.

Ferdie scowled at his sister and tucked a pencil behind his ear.

"Hey," cried Harper as she ran down to them, almost breathless with excitement, "I know where the cats are!"

"Where?" yelled Ferdie eagerly.

"Where?" whispered Liesel wistfully, for although Liesel didn't like cats, she did very much like adventures. The sight of a girl with a Scarlet Umbrella and a boy with a mist-colored wolf set her small heart pounding.

"The cats are at the Unforgotten Concert Hall," Harper half-yelled. "They've been captured by a man with magpie-feather hair."

"We must get them back!" cried Ferdie, shaking his fist. He closed his eyes in serious thought, only instead of a plan, he came up with a poem.

Liesel, however, sprang into action. "We must take every instrument we can carry, so we look like we're in a band. Then we walk inside and free the cats!"

Everyone turned to stare at her. Even Smoke looked impressed.

"Yes," they all agreed. "That's an excellent idea!"

Twenty minutes later, they were marching down the stairs laden with instruments. Harper had her cello on her back, a French horn in one hand, the Scarlet Umbrella in the other, and some maracas in her pocket.

Ferdie had his mother's button accordion around his neck and his tuneless recorder tucked through his scarf.

Liesel clutched Harper's clarinet, which was nearly as big as her and banged against her foot.

And Nate had his brother's Roman tuba in his arms and a tambourine fitted on top of his pork-pie hat.

Isabella, who had also agreed to help, strutted in front of them, the feathered wings of her samba outfit making her look like a butterfly.

This time, the stage door was open. Harper led her friends down a staircase of echoes, her heart beating with hope.

Isabella was to remain downstage and

pretend to be rehearsing a dance, while she was really keeping watch. The others were to hunt for the missing cats.

"Keep your instruments with you," Harper urged. "If anyone approaches, sound the alarm by playing three sharp notes. Music will be our secret signal."

The children scattered. Harper heaved her cello onto the stage. She thought of the many times she had sat in this very auditorium and imagined herself being part of the orchestra. Only, even in her dreams, Harper could never quite decide which instrument was truly for her. Each one held its own special wonder.

She looked around the edges of the stage but found only the rustle of the velvet curtains. No sign of the missing cats. She pulled her bow from her purple rain boots and began to softly play her cello.

Backstage, Nate was hunting through a box of props. Smoke sat at his side, her ears pricked like a guard dog's. Nate was so used to the dark that he worked quicker than anyone else. His fingers moved lightly over the floor and walls, studying the texture of the wood. The dampness in the floor. The depth of cobwebs. He could always tell how old a place was by the feel of its cobwebs, and this place was very old indeed.

Ferdie was in the dressing room staring at his reflection. He was a serious-looking boy, with a serious-looking scarf. He imagined the room full of actors, celebrating the opening night of his play. For how wonderful would it be to hear people speak the words he'd written? His skin began to tingle and his fingers twitched for a pencil. Before he could stop himself, he was scribbling down a sentence about a group of children in search of a mysterious cat.

Liesel was bored. She had searched the auditorium and found nothing but an old piece of candy. She wandered down a spiral staircase, Harper's clarinet banging against her foot.

At the bottom was a small wooden door that was ever so slightly open. On the door was a big brass sign saying KEEP OUT.

Everyone knows an adventurous child can never resist a forbidden door. And Liesel was no exception. Her eyes glittered brightly, and she scampered through.

Chapter Seven
THE THREE DOORS

The room on the other side was not very exciting at all, just a long dusty hall full of instruments. But as Liesel crept through it, she noticed something odd. All the instruments were tiny, almost small enough for a mouse.

Perhaps I'm in a story, she thought, *like*

the ones Papa writes, and she scurried on merrily.

Backstage, amid the velvet and dust, Smoke gave a low growl. Nate stood still and listened. From the stage he heard the rhythm of Isabella's feet and the haunting chords of Harper's cello. Farther off was the happy scrape of Ferdie's pencil. But where was the scruffy sound of Liesel? Nate raised the Roman tuba to his lips and played three sharp notes.

At once, Harper tucked her bow inside her purple boot. Ferdie tucked his pencil behind his ear. Isabella tucked her wings behind her back. They hurried to find Nate and quickly made a new plan. Isabella would stay on the lookout, while the others went to find Liesel.

Harper, Ferdie, Nate, and Smoke edged down the spiral staircase and through the forbidden door. Inside, the gleam of a tiny ukulele caught Harper's eye and she stopped.

She slipped off her cello and sank to the floor, her heart struck by its impossible beauty.

Ferdie stared at his friend and knew he had to help. He knelt down and took

Harper's hand. "You must let the ukulele go," he said in his most serious voice. For Ferdie knew what it was like to be drawn away by daydreams. He dreamed of words the way Harper heard music, Liesel longed for dark forests, and Nate for wild wolves.

Harper stared in surprise and let the ukulele clatter to the floor.

"Well done," grinned Ferdie. "Now, let's find my sister and those missing cats!"

Then a little shape that might have been a girl or might have been a mouse appeared at the end of the hall.

It was Liesel. She had found another door.

This door was much grander and made of bronze. It was also firmly locked.

Liesel kicked it, angry. "If only we had the key."

Nate ran his fingers over the lock. "Keys are too risky," he murmured. "They can get lost forever in pockets. Does anyone have a hairpin?"

"Liesel, there must be one in your hair—somewhere," Ferdie laughed.

Harper searched through Liesel's tangled locks until a hairpin was found.

Carefully, Nate slid the pin into the lock. He twisted it ever so slightly, put his ear to the door and waited for the soft sound of a click. As if by magic, the door sprang open.

"Genius!" cried Ferdie, throwing an arm around Nate's shoulders.

"Amazing, Nate!" Harper beamed as they tiptoed through.

Liesel could do nothing but gasp and gaze, her eyes wide with glee. She had never seen anything as splendid in her life. Nate was fast becoming the best person she had ever met.

The room they were in seemed to be full of sunlight, even though it was deep underground. The walls were lined with shelves, each stacked high with old music books.

"The Library of Long-Forgotten Music!" Liesel cried, jumping onto a shelf. It was a place every child in the City of Clouds had heard of, but didn't quite believe in.

Now it was Ferdie's turn to be stunned.

"The Library of Long-Forgotten Music!" he stammered. "It's here. It's real. We are in it." Oh, how he longed to sit down and write!

But before he had time to reach for his pencil, the bookcase Liesel was balancing on gave a sudden creak. Then the whole thing shifted, as if it were falling away from the world. Liesel gripped the shelf tightly,

her face alive with excitement. She had discovered yet another door!

With a shudder of amazement, the children and the wolf crept through. The door creaked closed behind them. The children stopped. They were in pitch-darkness, and for the first time they were afraid.

Chapter Eight
A STRANGE ORCHESTRA

Harper tried to step forward, but almost fell down a staircase.

"I should have brought my flashlight," huffed Ferdie.

"I should have been a mouse," fumed Liesel. "Then I could have found my way out."

"Aren't you forgetting something?" said Nate. The other children all fell still. "The dark's not a problem for me." He shrugged. "I'm used to moving through shadows as if they were sunlight." And with that, he tucked the Roman tuba under his arm and held out his hands to his friends.

"I'm so glad you're here," whispered Harper as Nate led them through the thick blackness, down the winding stairs.

In the darkness he was so comfortable in, Nate smiled. So few people understood that not being able to see could make you stronger in other ways. Or that having a wolf was very special, but also very ordinary. Most children were either too amazed or too terrified by Smoke to notice Nate. But Harper, Ferdie, and Liesel had changed that. For the first time, Nate's world held more than his mom and his brothers and midnight strolls with his wolf. For the first time, Nate's world held friendship and adventure.

A single eerie note of music fluttered from the shadows and the children stopped. Somehow, in the darkness, a maraca slipped from Harper's pocket, rattling to the ground like the sound of jittery nerves. Everyone tried not to laugh.

Then Harper crept down the final stairs and up to a small, filthy window. The others held their breath as she rose on her toes and squinted through. At once, she fell back pale-faced and gaping. Liesel and Ferdie sprang forward, fighting to get a look, while Nate helped Harper find her balance.

"The terrifyingly tall man is there," Harper whispered. "He's some sort of wild conductor. He's got an orchestra made entirely of cats!"

And it was true. As Liesel and Ferdie gazed through the dirt, they saw that crammed from floor to ceiling were cats of every color, all clutching tiny instruments. There were stray cats, pampered cats, wild cats, street cats. Cats that followed the path of the moon. Cats that only drank cream. Cats that once belonged to a witch.

"I think they're in a color code of fur," whispered Ferdie as he spotted his cat,

Ludo, thumping a big bass drum.

"They're in sections of an orchestra," hissed Liesel, staring at Snowflake, the ballet school cat, who was clasping a miniature viola.

"Yes!" whispered Harper. "Ginger cats on brass, black cats on woodwinds, snow-white cats on strings, and bright-eyed tabbies on percussion." And yet, Harper noticed that there were other odd instruments thrown in. Elsie Caraham's two cats, Memphis and Tallulah, were playing the bagpipes between them. Katarina, the Lucas family's cat, had a set of samba cowbells.

And there, in the middle of the room, was Midnight, in his paws a miniature mandolin.

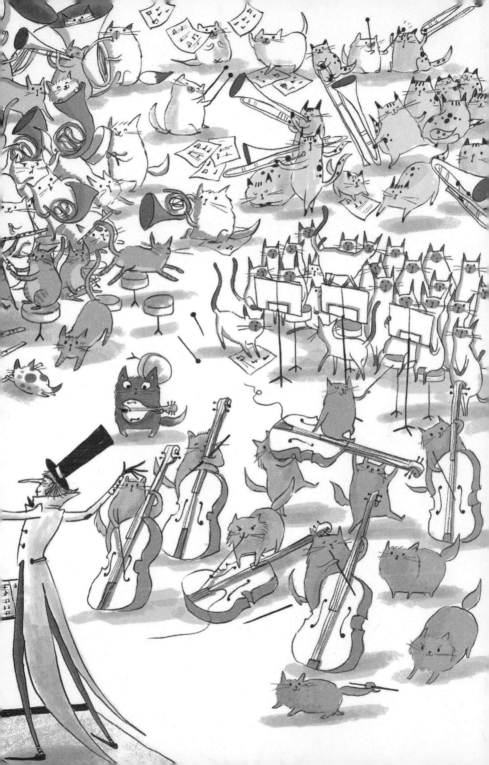

Then the orchestra began to play and Harper's heart was set on fire.

While the others listened in awe, Liesel did exactly what a mouse might do. She found a soft, dark gap between the panels of the wall and crawled through. Up and up she crawled until she was in the ceiling above the performing cats.

This is great, she thought proudly, *I'll drop down at the end of the song, grab Midnight, then free the other cats, and run.* But before Liesel had time to think any further, the ceiling gave way and she found herself slipping through the air.

Harper cried out in horror as Liesel fell from out of nowhere, knocking the Wild Conductor's hat across his eyes. He stumbled around in bewilderment, trying not to fall over the startled cats.

Liesel tumbled onto a family of large ginger toms. The cats shrieked, but Liesel fought them off with the clarinet.

"I'm going to get Midnight," Ferdie yelled, kicking the filthy window as hard as he could. As the window flew

open, Ferdie flew through it, diving at Midnight's feet and alarming everyone by playing a surprise chord on the button accordion.

Ferdie seized Midnight and the mandolin and threw them both to Harper.

"Midnight!" Harper cried, cuddling him close.

The Wild Conductor flew into a terrible rage and seized the nearest thing to him: a girl with tangled blonde hair. Liesel.

Chapter Nine
THE TERRIBLE THING

As Liesel was plucked from the ground, her fear turned to wonder. All her life, she had yearned to be a girl in a storybook, wandering through wicked forests. Now, an adventure had finally found her.

"Let my sister go!" yelled Ferdie, bashing the Wild Conductor with his tuneless recorder. Liesel pretended to scream in terror, while really, she was having the most wonderful time.

"What's happening?" cried Nate, who saw only a cloud of shadows and fur.

"He's gotten hold of Liesel," Harper stammered, her voice like a tremble of wind.

Then many things happened at once.

Nate bent down and whispered to his wolf. Smoke rose to her full size and, with a sickening snarl, she leaped. Ferdie fell back as the wolf soared through the window, teeth bared. The cats scattered like blossoms, their instruments crashing to the floor. The Wild Conductor stared at the wolf in shock, but he did not let go of Liesel. Instead, he held her in front of

him like a shield. Though Smoke growled

fiercely, there was no way she could attack

the Wild Conductor without harming the

child. And in that moment, Harper knew

the terrible thing she had to do.

"Wait!" Harper cried, her small body sagging with sorrow. "Let Liesel go and I'll give you back my cat."

The Wild Conductor sneered at her, "You don't even know what this cat can do."

Harper amazed everyone by answering back. "Why don't you explain?" she said calmly.

"He has an incredible musical gift," the Wild Conductor spat. "Without him the orchestra would be nothing."

"Of course he has a musical gift." Harper sighed. "I've taught him every instrument I know. But that doesn't mean he should be forced to perform in your orchestra."

The Wild Conductor's eyes glittered darkly. "He's quite happy performing," he said dryly. "It's the other cats that are the problem. They need him to lead them."

"Why do you need a cat orchestra?" demanded Ferdie in a seriously angry voice. "Fame? Fortune? Why?"

The Wild Conductor gave a low rasp of a laugh that made the children shiver. "No," he said crisply. "Because I can. Because I'm the best. Because when these cats play, there is a magic in the air that cannot be ignored. Their music could draw a storm from the sky, or summon a circus across many seas." For a moment, the Wild Conductor seemed lost in the greatness of his dream.

Then, with a sudden quickness, before anyone had time to move, he dropped Liesel and snatched Midnight from Harper's arms.

As Liesel sailed through the air, she noticed something silver in the Wild Conductor's sleeve. And just like that, as easily as a mouse might steal a crumb, she took it.

Then she landed in her brother's arms, causing the button accordion to squeak shrilly. The Wild Conductor stared at the children sourly and, with a swish of dark satin, he was gone, Midnight howling wildly in his arms, an orchestra of cats at his heels.

"Who is he?" Liesel gasped.

"Some sort of strange magician," said Nate.

Harper felt tears spilling down her cheeks. Ferdie slung her cello on his back and grabbed the Roman tuba.

Liesel pushed something small and silvery into her hand. Harper stared at it in shock and a smile spread across her face.

"Liesel, this is a conductor's baton," she cried.

"You can use it to get Midnight back," Liesel urged. "But you have to hurry."

Harper tucked the baton inside her purple rain boot.

"Go! Follow the cats. Run like the wind and you might just catch him," cried Ferdie, his face as serious as his voice. "Take Nate and Smoke with you. You'll be safe with a wolf and boy who's not afraid of the dark."

The children and wolf raced up the many stairs and out of the Unforgotten Concert Hall after the Wild Conductor.

Harper opened the Scarlet Umbrella and seized Nate's hand. "Ready?" she asked.

"Ready," said Nate and they sped into the City of Clouds.

As Harper ran, she felt weightless, as if she were made of nothing but sky and stars and evening breeze. She squeezed Nate's fingers tight and he quickened his step to match hers. Then their toes left the ground and they found they were running through twilight, their hearts lighter than the falling rain.

Chapter Ten
EDENTWINE

The Scarlet Umbrella drifted just high enough for Harper, Nate, and Smoke to follow the procession of cats who were making their way to the River North. But they were moving so quickly. More like rats than cats.

"We need to go faster," Harper muttered.

All at once, the Scarlet Umbrella flipped the children into the air, then spun upside down and caught them.

"Whoa!" cried Nate. "It's like we're in a boat."

"A boat that sails through the clouds," said Harper, laughing. "But we're still not fast enough."

Suddenly, Nate had an idea. He yanked a long pale strand of string from his pocket. "Edentwine!" Harper beamed, and hugged him.

Edentwine is incredibly long and incredibly tough. Woven from the stems of storm blooms, edentwine can't be broken by wind or rain.

At once, Harper brought the Scarlet

Umbrella down, so it hovered just above the ground. Carefully, Nate attached one end of the edentwine to Smoke's collar and tied the other to the handle of the Scarlet Umbrella. He ruffled the wolf's misty fur.

"Take us to the river, Smoke," he commanded. The wolf leaped forward quickly, pulling the Scarlet Umbrella behind her like a red kite caught on a wild sea breeze.

Harper clung to the side of the umbrella in wonder. She had only ever seen the city from the ground or the rooftop of the Tall Apartment Block. Now, she caught glimpses of it from between the clouds, and it stole her breath away. On every rooftop, storm blooms grew among puddles like water lilies, and train tracks crossed the city like a secret, glistening maze. In the starry darkness, Harper whispered all these sights to Nate. He smiled and held out his hands, feeling the texture of the clouds and rain on his skin. He laughed at its sweet taste and showed Harper how to tell a change in the weather by the feel of the wind.

Then they both fell silent. Below them, on the bank of the River North, was the sound of an orchestra of a thousand performing cats. Only the performance wasn't going very well. Memphis and Tallulah were fighting over the bagpipes. Snowflake had given up with the viola and Katarina and Ludo were curled up together having a nap. All around them, other cats struggled with their instruments. The only cat playing in time was Midnight. Harper gave a small smile. It seemed the Wild Conductor needed his baton.

"We've got something of yours," called Nate, holding up the baton.

The Wild Conductor looked furious.

"You can have this back in exchange for our cats," Nate said as casually as if he were talking to the milkman.

"Fine," the Wild Conductor replied. "You can have your cat back. But first, hand over the baton."

Any child who's ever heard a fairy tale knows you do not hand things over to terrifyingly tall men and trust them to keep their word. Harper and Nate were no exception, but they pretended to go along with the Wild Conductor's idea.

"Okay," said Nate, leaning over the side of the umbrella. He gripped the edentwine in his hands and pulled them down along it, until the umbrella hung in the air beside the Wild Conductor's face. Nate saw only the rough outline of a man edged in silver, but Harper saw something she hadn't spotted before. On his cloak was a tiny silver pin in the shape of a circus tent. Beneath it were the words: THE CIRCUS OF DREAMS. *What does that mean?* Harper wondered, noticing that the Wild Conductor's eyes held a glimmer of kindness. She crossed her toes in her purple boots and hoped their plan would work.

Nate handed over the baton and the Wild Conductor gazed at the children gravely. "You must understand," he said, almost sadly, "that I will never give up the cats. You see, I was once part of a wondrous circus, that I long to join again. These cats are my only way in. If I can lead a cat orchestra, then I can steal the show." Harper stared at his circus tent pin and, suddenly, she understood. The Wild Conductor wasn't bad or mean or dangerous; he was just a man chasing a dream, toward a runaway circus. A cat orchestra was, indeed, a brilliant thing, but he still had no right to steal people's cats. Harper gazed at Midnight's bright green eyes, and ever so gently, she brushed her hand against Nate's, giving him the signal. It was time to put their plan into action. Nate whistled shrilly and Smoke ran in a loop around the Wild Conductor's legs. At the exact same moment, Harper honked loudly in the Wild Conductor's face on the French horn.

Slowly, the Wild Conductor began to topple. In a dizzyingly fast flash, Midnight leaped from the falling man's arms and into the Scarlet Umbrella. Harper bent to kiss him. Nate snapped his fingers and in a swift and magnificent bound Smoke jumped in, too.

"Up!" Harper said, sending the umbrella twirling into the sky.

They'd done it! They'd saved Midnight.

They could rescue the other cats later, but

for now Midnight was free.

Harper's heart drummed with relief, and then it beat with terror. Part of the edentwine was still caught on the Wild Conductor's foot!

The Conductor took hold of it.

"Cut the twine!" yelled Nate, but Harper had no scissors and the wolf's teeth weren't sharp enough.

Nate gripped wildly at the knot around Smoke's collar and groaned. "It's too tight."

So they were stuck, halfway between the sky and the ground in a tug of war.

Chapter Eleven
HARPER'S GIFT

Harper thought desperately about what they could do. Then Great Aunt Sassy's voice came dancing from her memory: "Music is the magic that soothes the soul."

Harper set Midnight down and pulled her cello bow from her purple boot. She perched on the edge of the Scarlet

Umbrella and held the edentwine taut, then raised her bow and began to play it like a violin.

I'm not sure if you have ever heard edentwine played. But if not, imagine the sound of a skylark falling in love, and that will be near. Nate, Smoke, and Midnight were transfixed. Even the Scarlet Umbrella was frozen in time.

The Wild Conductor's eyes glazed over, as if he had entered a dream. "I see you have a marvelous gift," he muttered. Then he cleared his throat, straightened up, and yanked on the edentwine, pulling the Scarlet Umbrella from the sky.

All the while, Harper kept playing, feeling the notes from the world around her, and letting them find their way to her fingers and bow. As they neared the ground, the Wild Conductor tugged on the edentwine attached to Smoke's neck.

"No!" cried Nate, clinging to his wolf. Smoke was wild and fierce, but even she would be trapped by the unbreakable twine.

"Give me back the cat or I take the wolf," demanded the Wild Conductor.

Harper had no choice. Nate needed Smoke to be his protector. To warn him of the things he couldn't see. To growl if he stepped too close to the curb, or snarl if a stranger stepped too close to him. To stand with him in the dark, making everything brighter.

Nate locked his fists in anger. But

Harper spoke gently. "Cats belong to no one," she said, her voice soft, but clear. "They do whatever they choose, and this cat has chosen to be with me."

For a moment, the Wild Conductor's face flickered with doubt. Then he shook the thought away and, for the second time that day, snatched the cat from her arms.

Midnight hissed fiercely, but Harper whispered to him to be still.

As the Wild Conductor stepped free of the edentwine and Smoke gave an angry growl, Harper leaned out of the umbrella and called, "Don't worry, Midnight. I'm coming back."

The Wild Conductor scowled at her hatefully, but Harper held his gaze. She

knew now what she had to do, and the thought of it made her heart sing. She would use music. She would fight with her bow as if it were an arrow and fill the world with harmonies, night after night after night, until the stars shone with every note she played and the moon glowed with her sounds and the Wild Conductor saw that Midnight belonged with her. As the Scarlet Umbrella floated past the moon, Harper raised the piccolo flute to her lips and played Midnight's melody.

Gently, Nate's fingers unwound the edentwine from Smoke's collar. Nate felt her tense as if she were listening to something. He strained his ears, too. Then he heard it very faintly, blowing on the wind. Even though he couldn't see her face, Nate knew that Harper was smiling. It was the sound of Midnight's melody being played back to them from far, far below on a mandolin.

"Harper, your cat is trying to reach you," he breathed.

"That's what we have to do," Harper whispered. "We have to get the cat orchestra to follow me instead." And as the two tunes echoed through the night, a single glistening snowflake fluttered from the sky.

Chapter Twelve
THE MIDNIGHT MEETING

As the children and the wolf neared the
Tall Apartment Block, Harper gripped
Nate's hand in surprise. "There's a crowd
of people on the rooftop!" she whispered.

Isabella Lucas had raised the alarm and
told everyone about the children's courage,
about how they were planning to rescue

the cats of the City of Clouds, and about
how they were trying to outwit the Wild
Conductor. All the residents had rushed
to the rooftop and now they glanced up
at the Scarlet Umbrella, and a murmur
of hushes spread among them. Ferdie
punched the air, his thoughts filled with
poetry. Liesel scuttled around as if her heart
might burst. This was the proof she needed

that fairy tales were real. And one day, she would be the star of one. "We couldn't save Midnight. Or any of the cats," said Harper as she climbed out of the umbrella.

Peter stepped forward, his face full of pride. "But you tried your best, Little Harp," he smiled. Then he took Harper's hand and gazed upon her as if she were his own daughter. "We are here to help you," he said softly.

"Together we can get Midnight back, and the other cats will follow him," added his wife, Brigitte.

"We are at your command," gushed Madame Flora.

"You see, Midnight is no ordinary cat," said Elsie Caraham, peering at Harper with her unusually green eyes.

"Instruments," said Harper brightly. "We will fight with instruments."

All at once, the residents of the Tall Apartment Block flitted away like a flock of birds. Within a few minutes, they'd returned with a strange pile of instruments.

Brigitte carefully wound Great Aunt Sassy's sheets into a rope of lavender silk and tied one end to the umbrella's handle. Then Peter, Paulo, Mariana, and Madame Flora attached the instruments to the rest of the rope. There was a sparkling glockenspiel. A glistening triangle. An antique harpsichord. Harper's cello. And, right at the very bottom, the cherry-wood piano.

The clouds shivered and Icefall fell from the sky, making Harper blink.

"Don't worry," said Nate kindly. "You could do this with your eyes closed. I'll show you how."

Harper laughed and they leaped into the Scarlet Umbrella. With a whistle from Nate, Smoke bounded in, too, her eyes shining like icy stars.

"Good luck!" cried Ferdie, raising his fist.

"Strike the Wild Conductor down!" called Liesel.

"Be careful!" said Peter.

"Be brave!" said Isabella.

"Be you," said Elsie, giving Harper a wink.

Harper closed her eyes. "To the River North," she cried and the Scarlet Umbrella soared into the air.

Chapter Thirteen
THE WILD CONDUCTOR

On the bank of the River North, the Wild Conductor was fretting. Cats prowled around his ankles, pounding instruments in their small paws. They were very out of tune. The Wild Conductor sighed wearily. He was in a terrible mood. There was something very odd about the girl. The way she could make anything musical. The way she was calm and yet brave at the same time. The way she would not give up. He shook his head in annoyance. She was just a child after all. But a child with a mysterious gift.

A note of piano music silenced his thoughts. The Wild Conductor stared up and found himself gasping. Above him floated the Scarlet Umbrella, trailing a rope of lavender silk. At the bottom of the rope, silhouetted by the moon, sat Harper playing the cherry-wood piano. It was a wonderful song. A song of stars and mist and hope. A song that spread across the sky as if it came from the heavens.

Nate sank into the folds of the Scarlet

Umbrella, his arms wrapped tightly around Smoke. "This has to work, girl," he whispered, his ears listening hard.

Harper's music wove its way into the heart of every cat like a thread of moonlight and love.

Below her in the darkness, a mandolin began to follow. Then, almost as faintly as the rushing river, came the sound of bagpipes. Then the beat of a bass drum, the soft hum of a viola, and the chime of samba cowbells.

Every cat on the riverbank swiftly began to play, echoing Harper's song. It was like listening to magic.

"She's done it!" breathed Nate. "The cats are playing her tune." He stood in the

umbrella, raised a harmonica to his lips, and began to play along, Smoke howling triumphantly at his heels.

But it was not just the cats who were touched by Harper's gift. The clouds around the Scarlet Umbrella seemed to shimmer and glow, and then a flurry of coldness drifted through the air. Nate stood still and Harper almost stopped playing the cherry-wood piano. The little cold flakes were not Icefall or Heartbeat, nor any of the six rains of the City of Clouds. Nate laughed as one landed on his tongue . . . the little cold flakes were snow. "Your music is changing the weather!" he cried, and it was true, for the snowflakes didn't fall to the ground, they floated around Harper like a million frozen stars, enchanted by the tune she played.

The Wild Conductor felt his heart shake. He was losing the cats and he knew it. As he watched the child climb up and down the rope and play each instrument with breathtaking grace, surrounded by swirling snow, he finally understood. And he shuddered heavily. Harper was a girl with a musical gift far greater than his own. She could enchant the Midnight Orchestra and control the sky with just a single song. His cheeks burned with shame. *The cat and the girl belong to one another,* he thought grimly. It was as clear as the moon was bright.

With a reluctant flick of his wrist, he

released Midnight. High above the river, Harper and Nate felt the world shift. Snowflakes melted into a warm Heartbeat drizzle and they knew they had won. The cats of the City of Clouds were going home!

"You did it!" yelled Nate, twirling around in a wild umbrella dance. Harper whooped with joy, clambered up the lavender rope and joined Nate in the dance—an orchestra of cats playing just for them.

When the music ended, the Scarlet Umbrella glided down to the riverbank and Midnight leaped into Harper's open arms.

The Wild Conductor bowed his head. "I have done you a great wrong," he said,

almost sincerely. Then he cleared his throat
awkwardly and shooed away more cats.
Ludo ran past, looking quite the poet's
cat. Snowflake pranced by on pointe and

Katarina shimmied by on delicate paws. Two tabby cats with glinting green eyes purred around Harper's knees: Memphis and Tallulah. They were almost as old and wise as their owner, Elsie. Harper gathered them to her—they could come home in the umbrella as well.

"What will you do now?" Harper asked the Wild Conductor, settling herself in the Scarlet Umbrella.

"I will follow the River North," the conductor answered. "Perhaps I will raise a wolf. Perhaps I will find a magical cat. Perhaps I will train an orchestra of owls. That way, perhaps, I will again win a place in the Circus of Dreams. Who knows?"

He swept into a low elegant bow and with a twirl of black satin he was gone.

Harper turned to Nate and the two of them burst out laughing.

"What a strange man," said Nate with a shrug.

"I know," Harper chuckled.

She stroked Midnight's fur. "Home," she said happily, and as the moon glowed like the wolf's golden eyes, they sailed back to the Tall Apartment Block.

Chapter Fourteen
HOME

When the children arrived at the rooftop, news of the rescued cats had already spread. People were whooping and singing and laughing. Harper and Nate felt like heroes! They ran to hug Ferdie and Liesel.

"We did it!" Harper breathed.

"Yes, you did!" laughed Isabella, sweeping

all four of them into a hug.

Elsie Caraham held an empty glass up to the sky, and in no time at all it filled with fresh rainwater. "To Harper and her Scarlet Umbrella!" she cried, swigging down the rainwater in one large gulp. "To Harper!" echoed the other residents, raising teacups, mugs, and tankards to the sky and filling them with rain.

Harper clutched the umbrella's handle and let it lift her a little way into the air. She held up a teacup. "To Nate, Ferdie, Liesel, Smoke, and Midnight!" She beamed.

Applause broke out across the rooftop. The instruments were untied and everyone began to play.

This was not the music of concert halls

or theaters. This was music of the soul. Fast-beating fiddles, jaunty jigs on the piano, and mad melodies on the trumpet. A whirlwind of wild sounds filled the rooftop and echoed up to the twinkling sky.

Madame Flora pulled on her pointe shoes and seized Isabella's hands. Around and around they galloped, forming a dance floor beneath the storm blooms. Peter and Brigitte jumped up to join in, followed by Paulo and Mariana. Soon, everyone was singing and dancing and laughing and sipping fresh rain. Harper, Nate, Ferdie, and Liesel formed a circle and Nate taught them all the umbrella dance. It was the best party any of the children had ever been to.

Out of the corner of her eye, Madame Flora watched Liesel. She paid no attention to the little girl's knotted hair and muddy face. Instead, she took in the quickness of Liesel's feet and the lightness of her toes. *I wonder*, thought Madame Flora, beaming a quiet smile, *if this is the dancer I have long dreamed of finding.*

More residents wandered to the rooftop to sip the sweet, fresh rain. From the shelter of a deep-green umbrella, Nate's older brother, Noah, peered out. He watched the way Nate laughed and danced and held the hands of his friends. He watched the way Smoke sat slightly to one side, her ears pricked to the wind, her golden eyes fixed on the boy she loved most. He bent down to stroke her muzzle. "You and Nate are bound together by an invisible string of trust," he said to the wolf. "But it's okay for that string to stretch." Smoke gave a little yelp of understanding and Noah picked up a fiddle to play.

From across the rooftop, Elsie Caraham's bright-green eyes watched everything merrily. She took in the dancing and the party and the laughter of the children. Then her eyes came to rest on Ferdie and she smiled at the way that every so often he'd pull the pencil from behind his ear to jot things down. "So he's a writer," she mumbled to Memphis and Tallulah. "Well, perhaps I'll ask him to write my book." Elsie had always wanted to tell the story of her life, only it was packed so full of secrets. She would need someone very serious to help her. Someone with a very serious scarf.

Another sound rumbled through the clouds. The whirring sound of a helicopter. "Great Aunt Sassy!" Harper screamed, flying into her arms. "You're back early!"

"Harper, my darling girl! I missed you so much I thought my heart might break!" Sassy declared. She stroked Harper's hair. "And I see you've discovered the secret of the Scarlet Umbrella," she added fondly.

Harper giggled. There were so many questions she wanted to ask. But she didn't know where to begin. It had been a long night and, suddenly, she was very tired.

"Why don't you enjoy your party, you clever girl? You can tell me all about your adventures tomorrow," Great Aunt Sassy whispered.

As the stars grew fainter, the dancing slowed and the instruments were put away for the night. The children, the wolf, and the white-tip-tailed cat gathered under the

Scarlet Umbrella, chattering and laughing and gasping at the incredible adventure they'd had.

"Maybe we'll go on many more quests," said Ferdie, itching to grab his pencil and write them down, before they'd even happened.

"Next time, we have to come for the whole adventure!" cried Liesel, stamping her foot.

"We won't all fit inside the Scarlet Umbrella, though," said Ferdie. And because he was a poetic boy, he thought of a poetic plan. "We could fasten a cat basket below for Liesel. And I could attach my kite and fly above."

Nate pulled a strand of edentwine

from his pocket and all the children beamed. Harper yawned sleepily. She was still very tired. "Maybe not tonight," she said softly.

"Soon then," said Liesel.

"Soon," echoed the others.

And with that, the poetic boy, the mouse-like girl, the boy with the wolf, and the girl with an enchanted umbrella wandered inside the Tall Apartment Block—each of them shining with the glow of friendship and the dream of adventures yet to come.

"Goodnight, Midnight," Harper whispered. Midnight purred loudly, winked a green eye, and then the mysterious cat and the girl with the musical gift fell asleep, lulled by a song that seemed to come from the stars themselves.

In her dream, Harper sailed through the clouds in her Scarlet Umbrella, her star song echoing all around her. She saw a mysterious red-and-gold tent before her and she knew in her heart it was the Circus of Dreams. And she knew that one day she would go there.

About the Author

Cerrie Burnell is a presenter, actress, and writer, best known for her work in British children's TV. She was featured in the Guardian's 2011 list of the one hundred most inspirational women. She lives in the United Kingdom.

About the Illustrator

Laura Ellen Anderson is the creator of the Evil Emperor Penguin comic and the illustrator for many books including the Witch Wars series. She lives in the United Kingdom.